Boris Bad Enough

by Robert Kraus

illustrated by Jose Aruego and Ariane Dewey

Simon and Schuster Books for Young Readers

Published by Simon & Schuster Inc., New York

Simon and Schuster Books for Young Readers
Simon & Schuster Building
Rockefeller Center
1230 Avenue of the Americas
New York, New York 10020

Published by the Simon & Schuster Juvenile Division
SIMON AND SCHUSTER BOOKS FOR YOUNG READERS
is a trademark of Simon & Schuster Inc.
Manufactured in the United States of America

10   9   8   7   6   5   4   3   2   1   10   9   8   7   6   5   4   3   2   1 (Pbk)

Library of Congress Cataloging-in-Publication Data

Kraus, Robert, 1925–
  Boris bad enough.

  Summary: Boris' mother and father take him to a psychiatrist
when his behavior goes from bad to worse. The psychiatrist's
words are brief but effective.
  [I. Behavior—Fiction. 2. Elephants—Fiction] I. Aruego, Jose,
ill. II. Dewey, Ariane, ill. III. Title.
PZ7.K868Bo   1988   [E]   88-4636
ISBN 0-671-66894-3 H.C.   ISBN 0-671-66895-1 Pbk.

For Pamela, Bruce, Billy, and Juan

Boris was bad.

"I hope he doesn't get any worse,"
said his mother.
"He'd better not," said his father.
"Boris is bad enough!"

But Boris did get worse!

And worse. And worse. And worse!

His mother and father were at their wit's end.
So they took Boris to a shrink.

Boris kicked the shrink in the shins.

Boris's father yelled at him.
Boris's mother yelled at him.
Boris yelled back at them both.

"Quiet!" shouted the shrink.

"You are a bad father!"

"And you are a bad, bad mother!"

"And you, Boris, are a bad, bad, bad son!"

"What?" said Boris's father.
"Me bad? Impossible!"

"What?" said Boris's mother.
"Me bad, bad? Ridiculous!"

"What?" said Boris.
"Me bad, bad, bad?
Of course!"

And he kicked the shrink again.

**But on the way home,
what the shrink said sunk in.**

"I <u>have</u> been bad," said the father.

And he went home and tried to be good.

"I **have** been bad," said the mother.

And she went home and tried to be good.

"I <u>have</u> been bad," said Boris.

And he went home and he <u>was</u> good!

"Boris could be a little better,"
said Boris's father.

"Nonsense," said Boris's mother.
"Boris is good enough!"